Here We All Are

written and illustrated by

Tomie dePaola

A 26 FAIRMOUNT AVENUE BOOK

G. P. Putnam's Sons • New York

G. P. Putnam's Sons, a division of Penguin Putnam Books for Young Readers,
345 Hudson Street, New York, NY 10014. G. P. Putnam's Sons, Reg. U.S. Pat. & Tm. Off.
Published simultaneously in Canada. Printed in the United States of America.
Designed by Sharon Murray Jacobs. Text set in fourteen-point Garth Graphic.
Library of Congress Cataloging-in-Publication Data
dePaola, Tomie.
Here we all are / written and illustrated by Tomie dePaola.
p. cm. — (A 26 Fairmount Avenue book)
Summary: Children's author–illustrator Tomie dePaola describes
his experiences at home and in school when he was a boy.
1. dePaola, Tomie—Childhood and youth—Juvenile literature.
2. dePaola, Tomie—Homes and haunts—Connecticut—Meriden—Juvenile literature.
3. Authors, American—20th century—Biography—Juvenile literature.
4. Meriden (Conn.)—Social life and customs—Juvenile literature.
5. Meriden (Conn.)—Biography—Juvenile literature.
[1. dePaola, Tomie—Childhood and youth. 2. Authors, American. 3. Illustrators.]
I. Title. II. Series. PS3554.E11474 Z475 2000
813'.54-dc21 [B] 99-046747
ISBN 0-399-23496-9
1 3 5 7 9 10 8 6 4 2
FIRST IMPRESSION 4 - 00

For my sister Maureen and her family—
and my sister Judie.
I promise she'll "appear" in
one of these books.

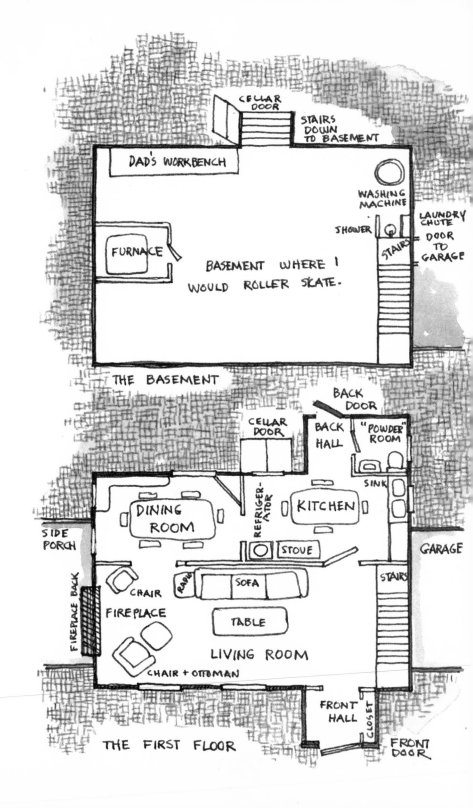

CELLAR
DOOR

STAIRS
DOWN
TO BASEMENT

DAD'S WORKBENCH

WASHING
MACHINE

LAUNDRY
CHUTE

SHOWER

DOOR
TO
GARAGE

FURNACE

STAIRS

BASEMENT WHERE I
WOULD ROLLER SKATE.

THE BASEMENT

BACK
DOOR

CELLAR
DOOR

BACK
HALL

"POWDER"
ROOM

SINK

SIDE
PORCH

DINING
ROOM

REFRIGER-
ATOR

KITCHEN

GARAGE

STOVE

STAIRS

RADIO

CHAIR

SOFA

FIREPLACE BACK

FIREPLACE

TABLE

LIVING ROOM

CHAIR + OTTOMAN

FRONT
HALL

CLOSET

THE FIRST FLOOR

FRONT
DOOR

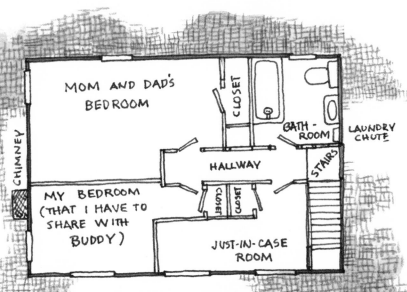

THE SECOND FLOOR

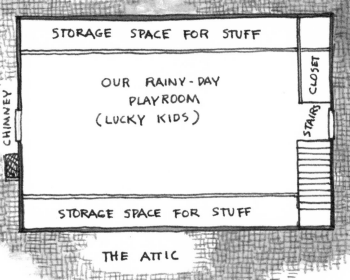

THE ATTIC

Chapter One

Have you ever moved into a new house? A whole house with a basement, a first floor, a second floor, and an attic? Well, when we moved from an apartment to our new house—our very first house—it was the greatest thing that had ever happened to me. At least up until then.

Here I was, standing in 26 Fairmount Avenue. I ran up the stairs and down, into the living room, the dining room, and all the bedrooms, all the way up to the attic and down to the basement. Then I ran up and down all over again.

Everything in 26 Fairmount Avenue was new! Well—almost everything.

"Nothing but the best for our new house!" Dad said.

"Our own house at last!" Mom said.

Our living room had a real fireplace. I tried sitting in the blue easy chair in front of it. The chair came with an ottoman-a big footstool to rest your feet on. But my legs were too short to reach it.

I looked up at the picture of a mountain at sunset that hung over the sofa. My dad's cousin had painted it and given it to us for our new house.

"What an artistic family," the neighbors would say when they came to visit. "So much talent!"

My mom's cousin was Morton Downey, the famous Irish tenor. My Irish cousins, the McLaughlin twins, were going to Pratt Institute, the famous art school in Brooklyn, New York. And there was the painter of the mountain, our Italian cousin, Anna.

The dining room was very fancy! We never ate there except for birthday parties and Special Occasions. Mom told us that every Christmas we would set out the Christmas village on top of the built-in sideboard. Then she opened the bottom drawer and showed us the Baby Book.

My brother Buddy and I each had pages with important facts written on them—our birthdays, how much we weighed when we were born, when we took our first steps, said our first words. Curls from our first haircuts were in a little pocket on a page. Even though Buddy and I had brown hair now, our baby curls were blond. Buddy's curl was almost white.

BUDDY
I YR. OLD
AUG. 31, 1931

TOMIE
I YR. OLD
SEPT. 15, 1935

I checked to make sure there were lots of pages in case we had any sisters. I already had a brother, and who needed two of those!

Mom loved her new gas stove in the kitchen. It had a clock, a timer, and places for salt and pepper shakers at the back, behind the burners. You set the dial for the oven to the right temperature, then turned it on and hoped it would light on its own. If it didn't, you had to put a burning match into a small space and light the gas. It made a *whoosh* sound when it lit.

Of course I wasn't allowed to light anything. There were stories about the lady who was too close and not fast enough with the match, and her eyebrows and eyelashes were burned right off! I really think it 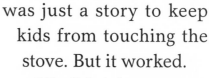 was just a story to keep kids from touching the stove. But it worked.

 We didn't have a new refrigerator, though. Mom and Dad liked the old "monitor top" one. It had a big, round drum on the top, which was the motor.

4

"This thing makes the fastest ice cubes in Meriden," Dad said.

Mom and Dad had new furniture in their bedroom. Mom had a fancy table called a "vanity," where she sat in front of a mirror on a little stool with a cushion and ruffles.

Mom would sit there to brush her hair and put on her lipstick. "This makes me feel silly," she said. "I'm not a movie star."

One day when no one was around, I sat there and put on my mother's lipstick, pretending to be Miss Mae West. She was my favorite movie star. When I tried to wash the lipstick off, I couldn't. So I got caught. I had bright-red lips for a few days!

Buddy and I had new furniture in our room, too—matching twin beds and a bureau with six drawers. I had the bottom three drawers because I was shorter.

"Your furniture is genuine maple," Mom told us. Maple?

When no one was looking, I licked the bedpost to see if it tasted like maple syrup or the maple candies we got sometimes. It didn't.

The bathroom, which was upstairs, was very special.

Before we moved in, my dad had told me there would be a laundry chute in the bathroom. It was to send the clothes, towels, and sheets that needed washing down to the basement, where the washing machine was. I was excited because in the movies I had seen people slide down curving chutes and land in piles of laundry. No such luck! Our laundry chute went straight down.

The bathroom had a real shower, but after just one shower, I wasn't allowed to use it. Something about getting water all over the floor and its dripping downstairs into the kitchen.

"Baths only for Tomie until he gets older," Dad said, mopping up the mess.

The bathroom was pink, black, and white. A band of white and then black tiles went halfway up the walls. The rest of the walls were painted pink.

I heard Mrs. Crane tell Mom, "Oh, Floss, you have such good taste. And you always have the latest things."

"I'm planning on putting up decals, too," Mom said.

"What are decals?" I asked. Mom explained that decals were pictures on paper. You soaked the paper in water and put the decal where you wanted it, rubbed gently with a cloth, then peeled off the paper backing, and there was the picture on the wall, the bed, or the bureau, wherever you had put it.

"Tomorrow we'll go down to Woolworth's and pick some out," Mom said. Woolworth's was the five- and ten-cent store and had everything!

Mom came to get me after kindergarten the next day and we went shopping. We looked through the decal book in the back of Woolworth's. I was getting all kinds of ideas. I looked at fruits and vegetables that had faces and arms and dancing legs, plain vegetables, and puppies and kittens and butterflies. I thought the dancing vegetables would look good in the kitchen.

But the sailboats and lighthouses and

seashells would be great in the bedroom I shared with Buddy. The mirror over our bureau looked like a ship's wheel. Uncle Charles said it was "nautical," so seashore designs were perfect.

"I don't think so," Mom said. "Not on all that brand-new furniture!"

Mom picked out decals with black swans and white swans and water lilies for the bathroom.

Then she surprised me. "Now, Tomie," she said, "let's look at decals for the baby's room."

"Baby's room?" I said.

"Yes." Mom smiled. "You know the little room that we said would be a baby's room just in case? Well, we're going to need it, because we're going to have a new baby in the family. Decals will make your old crib look nicer."

9

A sister! I thought. I couldn't wait.

"When will she get here?" I asked.

"She?" Mom said. "We don't know if it will be a new brother or a sister. You'll have to wait a little while, because it takes time for babies to be born."

Now that was going to be hard—even harder than waiting to move into 26 Fairmount Avenue.

When we got home, I ran right up the stairs and stood in the little "just-in-case" room.

"Please, please, please, Jesus, I want a baby sister," I prayed.

Chapter Two

We had only been in 26 Fairmount Avenue for a week when the Christmas vacation ended. It was time to go back to school.

I met my best friend, Jeannie Houdlette, at the corner. She lived just around the corner at 210 Highland Avenue. Her house was new, too. Now we could walk to school and back home together.

On the way we passed our old apartment on Columbus Avenue. No one had moved in yet. It was funny to see dark, empty windows without any curtains.

Carol Crane came running up to walk to school with us. She was older than I was, but younger than Buddy. She told me that her mom especially missed the Holy Water my mom would sprinkle on Mrs. Crane during thunderstorms so lightning wouldn't strike.

As soon as we got to our classroom, I went right up to my kindergarten teacher, Miss Immick, and told her that I had a new address.

"Well, aren't we a lucky boy," Miss Immick said. "Now you and Jeannie are neighbors."

Then Miss Immick clapped her hands to get our attention. "Boys and girls, today we are going to have a painting class."

That was great news for me. A whole year before, when I was only four, the relatives had asked Buddy if he knew what he wanted to be when he grew up. Buddy said he wanted to be Dick Tracy or Joe Palooka or Buck Rogers.

(Dick Tracy was a detective. Joe Palooka was a prizefighter. Buck Rogers was a spaceman. All three of them were comic-book characters. It sounded as if Buddy wanted to be a comic strip!)

"I know what I want to be," I had yelled out. And I did, too. "I want to be an artist when I grow up. I want to draw pictures and write stories for books and sing and tap dance on the stage."

I don't know if the other relatives believed me or not, but Mom and Dad, Uncle Charles, and my grandfather, Tom, all did. On my birthday and at Christmas, they gave me art supplies—paper, pencils, and crayons—and Mom took me to Miss Leah's Dancing School.

The only trouble about painting at school was Miss Immick's paint. She made it by pouring different colored powders into big glass jars and mixing them with water. The paint made the paper all wavy. When the picture dried, the paint rubbed right off.

Today Miss Immick made all the colors. Then she put a brush in each jar.

13

Then she said, "Now, boys and girls, we have to share, so let's be careful. Be sure to put the right brush back in the right jar of paint." She divided us into small groups. Little easels were set up all around the room. We put on old shirts of our fathers', or old aprons of our mothers', so we wouldn't get too dirty.

At least Miss Immick let us paint anything we wanted to, even if her paint wasn't so great. But sometimes she made suggestions.

Today she said, "I think if we all paint a nice scene with a tree and a house and the sun and some clouds that would be really nice."

I decided to paint a different picture, maybe a mountain like the one in the painting Cousin Anna did for our house.

Everything was going fine until someone in my group put the red brush in the green paint. Red and green are opposite each other on the color wheel. That means that when they are mixed together, they make a dirty, ugly brown color that looks like mud.

Great—now I'd have a hard time making my green mountain. I went over to Jeannie's group to borrow their green brush.

"We must stay in our groups," Miss Immick said.

"I'm just going to borrow the green brush for a minute," I told Miss Immick. I explained what had happened in my group with the red brush and the green paint.

"You know, Miss Immick, since I am going to be an artist when I grow up, I think it would be nice if I had my own paints and some better paper."

I know Miss Immick didn't think this was a good idea, because she just pointed at my easel and said, "Just go and finish your picture, young man."

That's why I had a picture of a muddy brown mountain in the rain instead of a beautiful green one in the sun to take home.

Chapter Three

Every afternoon in kindergarten we had to take "our naps." Everyone had his or her own little rug, or "mat," as Miss Immick called it.

The mats had big cardboard tags with our first names printed on them. If you had the same first name as someone else, Miss Immick put the first letter of your last name on the tag, too.

I don't think Miss Immick liked nick-names very much, because Johnny Gregory was John G. and Jack Rule was John R. and Jeannie Houdlette was Jean H.

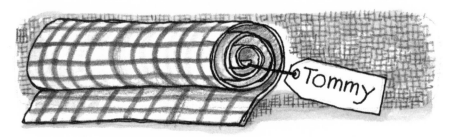

Even though I was the only Tomie, guess what? I wasn't allowed to spell my name T-O-M-I-E. I had to be T-O-M-M-Y. Miss Immick told me that T-O-M-I-E was the wrong spelling.

"But, Miss Immick, you say it exactly the same way," I had explained. Then I told Miss Immick that my mom's famous cousin, the Irish tenor Morton Downey, had given me the spelling of my name when I was just a little boy.

My mom had told Cousin Morton that I was sure to be famous when I grew up because I could draw really well and sing and dance, too. When I was three I had turned my sandbox over and used it as a stage. I danced even though I hadn't been to Miss Leah's Dancing School yet.

I knew all the words to the songs from movies starring Miss Mae West and Shirley Temple.

"Well, then, Floss," Cousin Morton said to my mom, "he's got to have an unusual spelling for his first name so people will remember it!"

"I don't care what your mother's famous cousin said," Miss Immick told me. "You should just be thankful that I don't call you Thomas. Now go and sit down."

For the next seven years I had to spell my name T-O-M-M-Y, even though my name was spelled T-O-M-I-E.

Anyway, this day when it was time for "naps," I thought I'd be helpful. I picked up Jack Rule's mat to hand to him.

But before I could, Miss Immick said, "Tommy, what are you doing!? You know you must never use any mat but your own."

We had that rule so we wouldn't get cooties, which are little bugs that can get in your hair. If you did get them, you wouldn't pass them on to anyone if you used your own mat every day. (If you did get them, it was awful because your mother had to scrub your hair with a special soap that made your whole head feel as if it was burning.) Every once in a while we had to take the mats home so our mothers could wash them.

"I was just being polite and handing Jack his mat," I explained. "In church on Sunday Father O'Connell said we should help each other."

"Well, all right, but don't do it again," Miss Immick told me.

20

I hated "naps." I wanted to be up and doing things. Gee, we could have used nap-time to learn how to read instead of waiting until first grade. I would lie there with my eyes wide open, thinking.

The next day I decided that it would be a good time to practice a new song I had learned. So, very quietly, I started singing to myself.

I felt a tap on my shoulder. I looked up. Miss Immick had her finger to her lips. She wanted me to be quiet. Then she motioned for me to get up and follow her out of the room.

We went to Miss Luby's office. Miss Luby was the school nurse. Miss Immick had me sit on the cot where you rested when you were sick.

"Tommy, what am I going to do with you?" Miss Immick said. "Why can't you be a good boy like your brother, Joseph?" (She didn't even call him Buddy.) "Now, I want you to promise me that you will try to behave. And not talk so much."

"I'll try, Miss Immick." But I knew it wouldn't be easy with all those rules.

Chapter Four

I wished that school with Miss Immick
could be like school with Miss Leah.

I had started dancing school
in September and I loved it.
My mom had taken
me there the year
before, when I was four.
But it hadn't worked out.

"What kind of danc-
ing do you like to do?"
Miss Leah had asked.

"Tap dancing—like
Shirley Temple," I
answered.

"How old are you?"

"I just turned four."

23

"Well, I usually have children wait until they're five before they take tap," Miss Leah said, "but let's see what you can do."

I stood there—waiting.

"Don't be shy," Miss Leah said.

"Oh, he's not," Mom told her. "Go on, Tomie. Show Miss Leah what you can do."

"I will when the music starts," I said. "I can't dance without music."

"That's it," Mom said. "I think maybe we should wait until next year. It'll be better for everyone."

So Mom had taken me back in September, when I was five. This time there were a lot of girls in the dance studio, too.

Miss Leah had lined us all up. She was wearing a short, swirly skirt and a blouse tied in a knot at her waist. Her shiny black hair was pulled back with a scarf. And she had on glittery silver tap shoes. She looked just like someone in the movies.

"Tomie, come and stand in the middle," Miss Leah said. "Face the mirrors, everyone, and watch what I am doing. *Up-back-down-up-back-down-slap-slap-up-back-down.*"

I couldn't keep my eyes off Miss Leah's silver tap shoes. Mine were black patent leather. The metal taps were on the toes and heels on the bottom of the shoes.

"All right, class, now you try it."

We all went *Up-back-down-up-back-down-slap-slap-up-back-down.*

"Very good," Miss Leah said. "Now let's try it with music."

A lady named Mrs. Anderson sat down at the piano. She began to play. Well, it was like the music told me just what to do! I loved it! *Dum-de-dum-de-dum.*

I'd go to Miss Leah's every Saturday. Another little boy joined the class. His name was Joey. We learned all kinds of steps—time steps, "shuffle-off-to-Buffalo," and things like that.

At our first class after the Christmas vacation, Miss Leah said, "Class, I am going to begin to teach you the dance number you will do in our recital at the end of the dancing-school year. It will be a military tap number."

"What's a recital?" I asked my mom on the way home.

"That's a whole show of all the children doing different numbers. Everyone wears costumes. There are scenery and lights—just like the movies," she answered.

Wow! I thought. *Just like the movies.*

I learned the steps quickly. Every week Miss Leah taught us new ones. We added those to the ones we had learned before.

27

Soon we would have the whole dance number learned.

The mothers all had little notebooks and they wrote down the new steps. My mom read the steps to me every night while I practiced. I was getting very good.

One Saturday in February Miss Leah taught us the drum roll. It sounded just like the *rat-a-tat-tat* of a drum. The class was having a hard time getting it just right.

I knew I could get it, so I closed my eyes and just listened to the sound of the taps Miss Leah made with her silver tap shoes, and BINGO—I got it! I could tell Miss Leah was pleased.

After class Miss Leah asked Mom and me if we would wait a minute and talk to her.

"You know, Mrs. dePaola, Tomie is doing so well that I'd like to give him something special to do in the recital. I can't give him a solo in the military number because that number is for the whole class to perform together.

"But I'm going to have a section of Mother Goose characters, and I'd like Tomie to do 'The Farmer in the Dell' with Joan Ciotti as the farmer's wife and Tomie as the farmer. I even have ideas for the costumes. What do you think?"

Mom looked at me. I held my breath. "Well, Tomie, it's up to you."

Up to me? Are you kidding? Just me and Joan Ciotti? Yes, yes, yes. After all, Joan Ciotti was a second-year student, and she even took private lessons.

"It will mean spending a little extra time here on Saturdays."

That was fine with me. The more dancing, the better!

After class the next Saturday, Mom and I stayed because Joan Ciotti and I were going to have our first practice together. Joan was a very good dancer and she told me that she was going to be a dancer when she grew up. So she was serious about it all, just like me.

Then I couldn't believe it. Miss Leah told me something else.

"Tomie, because you have such a good voice, I want you to sing a song in the recital, too. I'm not sure which song yet, but we'll talk about that next week. Now let's get started on 'The Farmer in the Dell.' I want you and Joan to try a few things."

I wasn't dancing with Shirley Temple, but Joan Ciotti would do just fine. I was on my way to becoming a STAR—singing and dancing on the stage.

Chapter Five

Our kindergarten class was going to put on a play for the whole school. We were going to do "Peter Rabbit."

I had played the part of John Alden, the pilgrim, in the Thanksgiving play we did for the first grade.

I didn't forget any of my lines or anything. The way Miss Immick smiled at me when she said "Peter Rabbit" made me sure that she was going to pick me to play Peter. I knew the story so well, and besides, Miss Leah said that I had "natural stage presence."

As much as I loved being on stage, my best friend, Jeannie, didn't. She was shy and very tall for her age. So I decided that Jeannie should play the part of the mouse who mumbles because she has peas in her mouth when Peter asks for directions out of Mr. MacGregor's garden.

She wouldn't have to remember any lines, just mumble.

I showed her how to puff out her cheeks and say, "Mumble, mumble, mumble."

Every day on the way home, we practiced. Finally the day for giving out the parts arrived.

"All right, boys and girls, let's bring our chairs into a circle." We each had a little colored chair with our names on a cardboard tag tied to the back, just like the "naps" mats.

Jeannie sat down next to me. I could tell she was nervous. I leaned over very quietly and whispered, "Now, when Miss Immick asks who would like to play the mouse, raise your hand and show how you can mumble. And don't forget..."

"Tommy, there you go, talking again. Won't you ever learn? Since you can't pay attention, you will not play Peter Rabbit. Peter will be played by Johnny Gregory. You will be Flopsy."

"But Flopsy is a girl," I protested.

"Not in our play!" Miss Immick said. "Now, boys and girls, I will read you the story."

Well, I was certainly disappointed.

I would be Flopsy along with Nancy Kiphut and Carolyn Kamens as Mopsy and Cottontail. We had to make our own rabbit ears and wear little red capes made out of stretchy crepe paper.

At dancing school, Miss Leah had told us how to act on stage. "When someone is talking or singing or dancing, be sure to look at them and react. That's one of the most important things to do when you are on stage."

That's what I'd do. Flopsy would react to everything that was going on with Peter. But I'd wait until the real performance and not do anything when we were just practicing. It would be a surprise!

So in front of the whole school—the students from all the grades; the teachers; Miss Burke, the principal; Miss Philomena, the school secretary; Miss Luby, the nurse; and Mr. Walters, the school janitor—and our parents, Flopsy reacted.

When Peter went into Mr. MacGregor's garden and he wasn't supposed to, I clasped my hands in shock.

Every time Peter did something, I did something, too. I waved my arms around. I covered my eyes. I put my hands over my ears. I opened my mouth wide in surprise.

I could hear the audience laughing. The grown-ups even clapped a couple of times.

When it was over, Flopsy had stolen the show. Jean Minor was great as Mrs. Rabbit. Jack Rule was scary as Mr. MacGregor. Jeannie was wonderful as the mumbling mouse with peas in her mouth. Johnny Gregory was okay as Peter. But I was the hit of the play!

Miss Mulligan, the fifth-grade teacher who played the piano at our auditorium shows, came up to me and said, "Well, Tommy, you certainly know how to steal the show. You're a real ham!"

I looked over at my mom. She waved. *How proud she must be*, I thought. Miss Immick didn't say much, except, "Boys and girls, you all did a very nice job." She didn't say anything special to me. I supposed she was sorry that she hadn't asked me to be Peter Rabbit after all.

Our parents all came into the kinder-garten room to take us home.

"Well, Tomie," my mom said, "that was quite a performance."

I smiled a big smile.

"I think you owe Johnny Gregory and Miss Immick an apology. It wasn't very nice of you to take all the attention. After all, you were just one of the bunnies, not the star. So tomorrow you'll say you're sorry to Johnny and Miss Immick. Okay?"

I looked down at the floor and nodded.

Jeannie came over to say hello. "Jeannie," Mom said, "you were perfect. Congratulations."

"Tomie showed me how to do it," Jeannie said. "He should have been Peter."

The next day at school I said I was sorry to Miss Immick and Johnny Gregory. I did it when no one else could hear me, though. I guess I was only a little sorry.

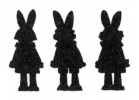

Chapter Six

One afternoon in February I saw my mom sitting in the principal's office. Our class was on our way back from the "lavatories," or boys' and girls' rooms. She didn't see me.

When we got to our room Miss Philomena came in to watch us while Miss Immick went to a "meeting" in Miss Burke's office.

The bell rang to announce that school was over for the day. Miss Immick hadn't come back. Miss Philomena said I was to wait.

Buddy came into the kindergarten room.

"Boy, are you in trouble," he said. "Mom is here having a meeting about you! We have to wait so we can all go home together.

Are you going to get it!" Then he sat down with a smirk on his face.

What did I do now? I wondered.

I had apologized for "Peter Rabbit," so that couldn't be why Mom was here.

Was it for my singing during "naps"?

Was it for my waiting for my mom inside the school building to go to Woolworth's instead of waiting outside, where we were supposed to wait? But that was way at the beginning of the year.

Or was it for telling all the teachers that my mother was so smart that she could stand on her head? Maybe they had asked her to come in and show them.

What could it be?

Suddenly I heard Miss Burke talking out in the hall. "Well, thank you for coming in, Mrs. dePaola. I'm sure you can take care of everything."

Oh, boy, here it comes! I thought.

Then I heard Miss Immick's voice. Was I surprised at what she said!

"Tommy is really a very good boy —different from his brother—

a little too talkative, but so interested in everything. He's a joy to have in class," she ended.

"Yeah, I bet!" Buddy piped up.

My mother popped her head in and said, "Okay, boys. Let's go."

Buddy poked me.

"What did Miss Burke say about Tomie?" he asked my mom.

"Never you mind," Mom said. That's all she said. I was very nervous. When was I going to get it? Probably at home.

When we got there, Mom told Buddy to go outside and play. I could tell he wanted to hang around to see me get it.

"Now, Tomie, I know you are wondering why I was at school today. I want you to know that Miss Immick told me that she thinks you talk a little too much, but that you are smart and creative. That was the first reason for the meeting.

"The second is that there is going to be a big Valentine's Day party for the two kindergartens and the two first grades. Miss Immick asked me if I would make the valentine cookies and sheet cakes for the party." (My mom always made sheet cakes for our birthdays. They were huge cakes, one layer high, made in a big, flat pan. They were so big that we'd take them to school for the whole class.)

"The party is going to be held in the hall-way between the classrooms. The teachers want to have a valentine mailbox. Instead of one in every room, they want a big one for all the kindergarteners and first graders to use together. It will be put on a table across from Miss Burke's office, right at the main entrance to the school.

"Now for the big reason for the meeting. They want *you* to make it! What do you think?"

Well, I almost fainted—first from knowing that I wasn't going to get it, and second because it was such an honor!

"Can you help me?" I asked.

"Of course," Mom said.

The next few weeks were pretty exciting for me. I asked my grandfather, Tom, for a big cardboard box from his grocery store and some of the shiny white paper he wrapped the meat in to cover it.

Mom helped me glue on the paper very neatly.

Then we went to Woolworth's and the new five- and ten-cent store, Kresge's, for red construction paper, ribbon, and shiny stick-on hearts. We even bought a package of white paper doilies that looked like circles of lace. I made drawings of cupids and doves. I cut them out and pasted them on the sides.

I worked hard on that valentine mailbox. My dad cut a slot in the top for the cards to go through, and we made sure the bottom could open and close. My dad said they would probably want to use it again, so I should make it as sturdy as possible.

Dad was right. They used that valentine box the whole time I was in elementary school.

The party was great. We all wore party hats. "Mailmen" passed out the valentines. (I made all of mine myself.) Mom baked four delicious sheet cakes with pink frosting and little heart-shaped candies with messages on them. The cookies were heart shaped, too, with red and white icing and little silver sprinkles on some and cinnamon candy hearts on others. We had pink punch, and by the end of the party, everybody had red lips and tongues.

All the grown-ups admired the valentine mailbox and told me what a nice job I had done.

Mrs. Bowers, the art teacher who came to visit our school every so often to give art lessons, happened to be there.

"Well," she said, "I can't wait to get *you* in art. We'll have a good time together."

I got real excited about that! But I'd have to wait until second grade for art lessons with Mrs. Bowers.

Miss Immick looked very proud of me. (I had made a special valentine for her with lots of little windows to open and lace doilies glued inside.) "It's one of the nicest valentines I have ever received," she said. "Thank you, Tommy."

From that day on, Miss Immick and I got along really, really well. I guess she was a good teacher after all!

Chapter Seven

The time for the new baby was getting close. Mom let me put my hand on her tummy so I could feel the baby kick. I whispered, "Hello, baby sister."

Mom told me again for the fortieth time that we couldn't be sure if the baby would be a boy or a girl. But I just told her that I wanted a baby sister with a red ribbon in her hair.

Mom was busy getting the just-in-case room ready. Dad and Buddy painted it yellow. I made pictures to hang on the walls.

I went to Perlin's store with my mom to buy nightgowns, booties, and tiny sweaters. All the clothes looked like doll's clothes. (When Jeannie saw them, she told me to tell

my mom that we could borrow her
Dy-Dee Doll's clothes if we wanted to.)

Then Mom bought something
that made me laugh—
"Belly Bands" that wrapped
around the baby's tummy.

"They must be to keep
the baby's belly button from
falling off," I said. Mom laughed, too.

Next we went to Woolworth's and bought
decals to decorate the baby's crib. I picked
out ones just right for a baby sister.

She was going to have such a pretty room. I saw Mom buy some other ones, just in case it was (please, no) a baby brother.

On the way home Mom told me that when it was time for her to go to the hospital, Aunt Nell would come and take care of Buddy and me while my dad went to work. He had an important new job in Hartford as the State Barber Examiner. (This meant that he had to go all over Connecticut visiting barbershops to make sure they were clean and followed all the health rules.)

I loved Aunt Nell. She was my grandfather Tom's sister and lots of fun. Whenever she took care of Buddy and me for my mom, we would all have tea with milk and sugar and a plate of crackers and peanut butter. She also made great hamburgers with meat from Tom's grocery store.

But something happened that changed everything.

Nana Fall-River came to Meriden. Nana Fall-River was my Italian grandmother. I called her that because she lived in Fall River, Massachusetts. She was on her way to visit her daughters, Aunt Kate and Aunt Clothilde, in the Bronx in New York City. But she wanted to stop in Meriden to see our new house.

When Nana Fall-River arrived, she walked in, took off her hat and coat, opened up her big black purse, took out her apron and put it on. She went straight to the kitchen without even looking at the house.

Nana Fall-River always traveled with her apron and lots of food.

(Nana Fall-River thought that Mom didn't cook right and that my dad must be starving to death. He wasn't, of course.)

Uncle Nick had driven Nana Fall-River over from his house, where she was staying with him and Aunt Loretta. I had a picture in my head of Nana Fall-River in the back of the car surrounded by pots and boxes of food.

I watched as Aunt Loretta and her daughter, my cousin Helen, carried in all the food— first the big pan of spaghetti sauce, which Nana Fall-River called "gravy," with meatballs and lots of other stuff in it. (We children were never allowed a meatball when we went to Nana Fall-River's house. Meat was for grown-ups.)

Then they carried in jar after jar of tomatoes and peppers, big cans of olive oil, and other things Nana Fall-River had made. She even had loaves of Italian bread from the bakery near her house in Fall River.

"You didn't need to bring bread, Ma," Dad said. (It was funny hearing my dad call Nana Fall-River "Ma.") "We have a really good Italian bakery right on Lewis Avenue—Bonazinga's."

"It's not-a like-a Marzilli's," Nana Fall-River answered.

Nana Fall-River also brought all kinds of cookies, which grown-ups liked but we didn't. They were hard as rocks and had a funny flavor like licorice.

Oh, brother, I thought. *I guess it is spaghetti and tomato sauce for dinner. No meatballs for Buddy and me.*

My mom didn't even bother to go into the kitchen to help, but my dad went in and put on the white apron that Tom had given him.

The kitchen was off limits to Buddy and me, so I sat and talked to Cousin Helen about dancing school. She was a lot older than I was and a very good tap dancer. I showed her what I was learning at Miss Leah's.

Finally dinner was ready. Nana Fall-River handed me a plate of spaghetti, real thick strands, not thin like Dad always made. This "macarone," as Nana Fall-River called it, was like the stuff Mom used to make macaroni and cheese. But they weren't short pieces like Mom's. They were long, like regular spaghetti, but thick, with big, round holes. My dad called them "sewer pipes."

My plate was piled high, but not a meatball in sight.

"Mangia, mangia—eat, eat," Nana Fall-River said. So I started in. At least here at 26 Fairmount Avenue I wouldn't have to clean my plate. In Fall River, my grandmother was the boss and we had to do what she said. Even Mom couldn't help us when we went to Nana Fall-River's house. But I knew that Mom would come to the rescue at 26 Fairmount Avenue.

Buddy dug right in. "He has such a good appetite," everyone would say.

I was supposed to be a "picky" eater. The truth is that I liked to eat. I just didn't like some things. But I liked other things that kids aren't supposed to like, such as spinach—especially the way Mom cooked it, with lots of butter and a little sprinkling of vinegar.

A few days later we were coloring eggs for Easter when the phone rang. It was Uncle Nick. Aunt Kate wasn't feeling so well, so Nana Fall-River wouldn't be going to the Bronx. She was staying in Meriden for a few more days.

When Buddy and I woke up on Easter Sunday, we found Easter baskets from the Easter Bunny.

We got dressed up to go to church. I had a brand-new pair of brown-and-white saddle shoes. Buddy had his first pair of long pants.

Uncle Charles and his girlfriend, Viva, stopped by with their friend Mickey Lynch. Viva had on a fancy hat. "My Easter bonnet," she said. Uncle Charles and Mickey Lynch were all dressed up, too. "Because you'll be staying here for Easter dinner," Uncle Charles said, "I brought these two presents the Easter Bunny left in Wallingford."

He gave us each an enormous chocolate bunny.

"Aren't we going to Tom and Nana's?" I asked.

"No," Mom told us. "Nana Fall-River has already cooked a big dinner for us."

Oh, well.

The next day, Mom seemed awfully busy. "I think the new baby will be coming soon," she told me.

I took some of the green cellophane grass from my Easter basket. I put a colored egg and a marshmallow on it.

"For my baby sister," I said. "The one with a red ribbon in her hair."

"We'll see," Mom said. "We'll see."

Chapter Eight

That hat night while Buddy and I were asleep, Mom and Dad went to the hospital and the baby was born.

The sun was just coming up when Dad came home and woke me up. "Tomie, you have a new baby sister!"

I should have been the happiest little boy in the world. But I wasn't.

When I got out of bed Mom wasn't there, but Nana Fall-River was. For breakfast she gave me a piece of Italian bread that she had toasted on top of the stove.

"Mom gives me Rice Krispies," I said.

"This is good," Nana said.

"Can I have some butter and jelly on it?" I asked.

"No."

"Can I go to Jeannie's house?" We didn't have school that week.

"You stay here."

"Can I go out in the yard and play?"

"No."

"Can I listen to the radio?"

"No."

We had a brand-new Zenith radio in the living room, and Mom let me listen to my favorite programs—"Let's Pretend" and "Jack  Armstrong." It had a round glass dome covering the station numbers and buttons to push to change stations instead of a dial.

Now Nana wouldn't even let me listen to the radio.

I went upstairs to the attic. It was our rainy-day playroom. But it wasn't raining today.

I sat on the window seat and looked out. I could see more houses being built. I could see West Peak and the stone tower called Castle Craig. I could see Hemlock Grove, the place where most of the big hemlock trees were knocked down during the Big Hurricane of 1938.

I stayed up there all day waiting for my dad to come home. It was almost dark when I saw him drive up and park the car. I raced down the attic stairs, then the front stairs, and out the front door.

I didn't even let him get inside before I asked, "When is Mom coming home?"

Before he could answer, Nana called out from the kitchen that supper was on the table. We went in and sat down. More sewer pipes.

I asked Dad again, "When is Mom coming home?" He started to talk, but Nana interrupted and started spouting in Italian. Then she looked at me and said what she always said: *"Mangia, mangia."*

Something was fishy. After supper I went upstairs and got into bed. Dad came in and sat on the edge of the bed. "Tomie, I know you miss Mom, but she has to stay at the hospital with your baby sister for a little while. Then they will come home together."

Then he told me not to talk to Nana about Mom and my baby sister.

60

"Nana's from the Old Country," Dad said. "They don't mention a new baby until it has been taken to the church and baptized." (That's when the baby gets its name.)

So *that's* what they had been talking about at supper.

"When *will* Mom be coming home?" I asked.

"In about ten days," he said. Ten days seemed like forever to me. In those days, mothers spent at least that long in the hospital with their new babies.

"Can I go and see Mom?" I asked. Dad explained that I couldn't because children under twelve weren't allowed in to visit.

"When is Aunt Nell coming?" I asked.

"She's not coming," Dad said. "Nana Fall-River's going to stay and take care of you instead."

I almost cried. Aunt Nell would have read to me. She wouldn't have talked to my dad in Italian all the time. And she would have let me talk about Mom and my baby sister. And she would have fed us hamburgers!

"Now go to sleep and be a good boy," Dad said.

But I wasn't a good boy. I just couldn't help it. I wouldn't eat. I wouldn't sleep. I wouldn't even go to the bathroom. I just wanted my mom and my new baby sister. And I wanted Nana Fall-River to go home!

On Saturday Dad took us to Wallingford to visit Tom and my other Nana at their grocery store.

I told Tom that all I wanted was a hamburger. He made me a cold cut sandwich with mustard and mayonnaise on soft white bread. It was delicious!

As the week dragged on, I got worse and worse. Mom told me later that every night when Dad went to visit her in the hospital, he'd say, "Guess what Tomie did today?" I was a BIG problem.

But Mom knew how to solve the "Tomie" problem. I found out the first day we went back to school.

The hospital was right across the street. As I was walking up King Street on the way home, I heard a voice calling, "Tomie, Tomie, up here."

I looked up and there was my mom, calling to me and waving.

I waved back. Then I stopped all the kids going by and said, "Look! Look! There's my mom. We just had a new baby sister!"

Well, Mom talked to me and told me that my baby sister was beautiful and that they would be home soon. She asked me to be a good boy, to help Nana, eat my dinner, and stop causing so much trouble. "And please, go to the bathroom."

That was all I needed. I was so happy that I ran all the way home.

"Nana! Nana Fall-River! I saw Mom and talked to her. She was looking out of the window. She is going to be home soon—with you-know-what! Nana, I'll be a good boy. Let's be friends!"

Nana Fall-River gave me a big hug.

"My friend!" she said.

That night I ate all my sewer pipes. I fell asleep and, yes, I even went to the bathroom. Dad was happy, too. And guess what? The next night he cooked hamburgers for Buddy and me.

Nana Fall-River even ate one!

Chapter Nine

Mom was coming home!

Tom and Nana, Uncle Charles, his girlfriend, Viva, Aunt Nell, Nana Fall-River,
and, of course, Buddy were there waiting
with me.

When I heard the car
stop in front of the house,
I hid behind the big
blue chair. Mom came in.
"Where's Tomie?" she asked.

I jumped out. "Here
I am!" I shouted.

"Come and look," Mom said.

There she was. My baby sister
with a red ribbon in her hair!

Mom had made Dad stop at Woolworth's on the way home to buy the ribbon.

I got to sit in the armchair and hold the baby very carefully. Nana Fall-River showed me how. It was great!

My baby sister was going to be given her name at the baptism at St. Joseph's Church on Sunday afternoon. Her name would be "Maureen." My mom told me that "Maureen" meant "little Mary."

The Irish family baptism gown was taken out of the box in the attic. It was a long white dress with lace and ribbons. There were cotton petticoats and flannel ones, too, and in case it was cold, a little jacket and a bonnet.

The gown had been made by my great-grandmother, Nana Upstairs, for my mother's baptism. Then Uncle Charles wore it, then Buddy, then me. Now Maureen would be wearing it.

In those days, the mothers didn't go to the church for the baptism. And, of course, no one but me thought it was a good idea for me to go.

I had been to one baptism when I was a little boy—maybe two years old. My mom and dad were going to be godparents and since NO ONE wanted to baby-sit me (I screamed a lot when my mom wasn't there), Mom and Dad took me with them. The story goes that I sat there very quietly until the priest poured water on the baby's head.

"I want water on my head, too," I cried.

The priest said, "Little boy, if you're quiet you can have anything you want after the ceremony."

"Big mistake, Father," my dad said. I *was* quiet until the ceremony was over.

"Now, little boy," the priest asked, "what would you like?"

67

"Baby Jesus," I answered. I guess I wanted the figure of the Baby Jesus I had seen in the manger scene at Christmas.

Well, I caused quite a fuss when I didn't get it. But, the next day, my mom took me to Woolworth's. They had started putting out the Christmas stuff, so Mom bought me my very own Baby Jesus figure, and I stopped being such a pain.

So for Maureen's baptism I had to stay at home with Mom, Nana Fall-River, and Buddy while the godparents—Mickey Lynch and Cousin Helen—went to St. Joseph's with Dad.

Relatives and friends started to arrive at 26 Fairmount Avenue—Nana and Tom, Uncle Charles and Viva, Aunt Nell, Cousin Mabel and her husband, Bill Powers, Uncle Nick and Aunt Loretta, Carol Crane and her mother and father, and a bunch of other friends and family.

We were having a big party. Of course.

When Cousin Helen and Mickey Lynch came in with baby Maureen, everyone clapped. Nana Fall-River was so relieved, I think. Now she could relax. The baby was baptized.

"Tomie," Mom said. "Sit in the blue chair. You're going to hold your baby sister for the home movie. Remember how?"

Of course I did!

I was so proud, and Maureen looked so pretty in her long white dress. I had lots of plans for her.

Here we all are. Our family is bigger and our house at 26 Fairmount Avenue is much bigger than the old apartment on Columbus Avenue—and much better for new babies, parties, friends, and relatives—and new adventures.

But more about all that later!

The End